Jazzy Miz Mozetta

Brenda C. Roberts   Pictures by **Frank Morrison**

FARRAR STRAUS GIROUX / NEW YORK

For Loubertha, the original Lightnin' Lou
—B.C.R.

For my daughter, Nia "Super Boo," and my sons, Nyree "The Builder,"
Tyreek "The Comic," and Nasir "The Baby"
—F.M.

Text copyright © 2004 by Brenda C. Roberts
Illustrations copyright © 2004 by Frank Morrison
All rights reserved
Distributed in Canada by Douglas & McIntyre Ltd.
Color separations by Chroma Graphics PTE Ltd.
Printed and bound in the United States of America by Berryville Graphics
Typography by Nancy Goldenberg
First edition, 2004
3 5 7 9 10 8 6 4 2

www.fsgkidsbooks.com

Library of Congress Cataloging-in-Publication Data
Roberts, Brenda C.
    Jazzy Miz Mozetta / Brenda C. Roberts ; pictures by Frank Morrison.— 1st ed.
        p.   cm.
    Summary: On a beautiful evening, Miz Mozetta puts on her red dress and blue shoes
and dances the jitterbug just like she did many years before.
    ISBN 0-374-33674-1
    [1. Dance—Fiction.   2. African Americans—Fiction.]   I. Morrison, Frank, 1971– ill.
II. Title.

PZ7.R5397 Jaz 2004
[E]—dc21

                                                                                        2002026508

"An extraordinary evenin', if I do say so!" Miz Mozetta threw open her parlor window and smiled at the fat yellow moon. "I believe I'll take a stroll."

"But first, a little Pretty Plum powder. Now a little Tango Mango lipstick."

Miz Mozetta looked over her flock of bright dresses. "Hmmm. Let me see.
I declare I feel like red tonight."

She chose one the color of July firecrackers. "My best color, if I do say so."

Her pizzazzy hat was from a shop way uptown. "Now, *this* hat is *sayin'* somethin'."

Last of all, she slid her feet into her fancy blue shoes—old favorites. "Skiddle de wee bop she bop . . . yeah!"

She strutted down the stairs, humming something snazzy.

Outside, Miz Mozetta's good old friends were enjoying the moonlight. "Hey, Miz Mozetta!" called Mister Willie. "Lookin' jazzy tonight!"

"Hey back at ya." Miz Mozetta winked her long lashes. "I do look jazzy, don't I?"

"Sit down and play some checkers," said Mister Brown.

"Sit down and let me tell you what the butcher said the baker said the grocer told the barber," said Miz Lou Lillie.

"Sit down and sip some lemonade," said Mister Willie. "It's sweet *and* sour. Mighty tasty."

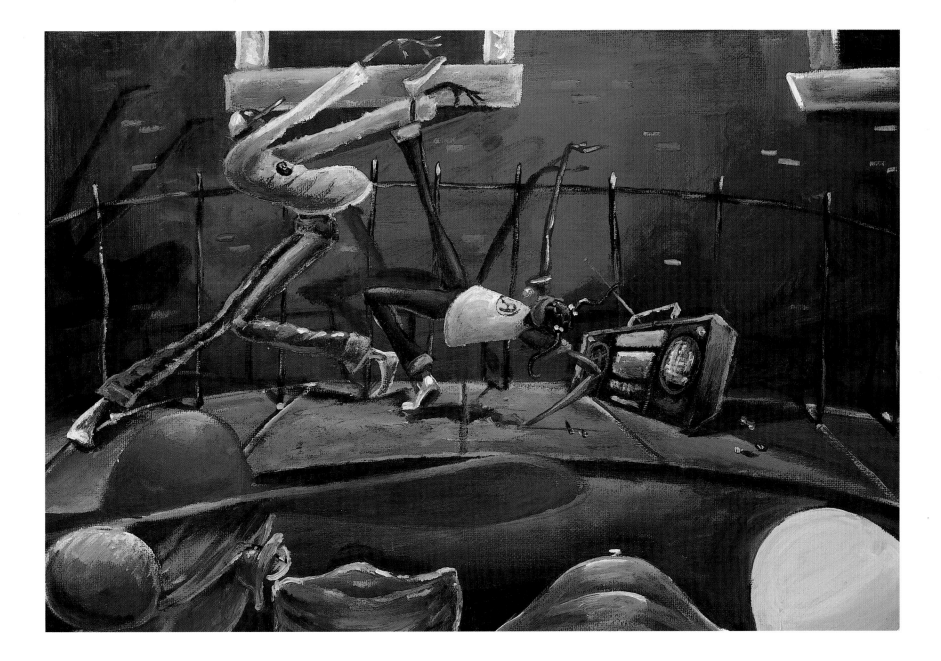

But Miz Mozetta was not listening. A crazy beat was thumping in her good ear. It was coming from across the street, where her young neighbors Cap and Rudy were dancing.

"Mm. Makes me want to dance, too," Miz Mozetta said. Her foot began to tap. "Come on, Mister Brown, let's cut a rug!"

Mister Brown would not budge. "Not me, Miz Mozetta. My dancin' days are done, honey dear."

Miz Lou Lillie said she had a sore toe.

Mister Willie said he had a crick in his neck.

Miz Mozetta stamped her big blue shoe. "Shucks!" she pouted. "I can't let all this sweet moonlight go to waste."

She gave her hat a pat and sashayed across the street. "Hey there, chickadees!" she called to Cap and Rudy. "Got room for one more?"

Cap and Rudy stopped and looked Miz Mozetta up and down.

"Can you do this?" asked Rudy. She did the splits and shimmied back up.

"Or this?" Cap jumped as high as Miz Mozetta's hat.

"Hmmm," Miz Mozetta said.

"Tell you what," said Rudy. "If you sit over there with your friends, we'll show you all our moves."

"But . . ." said Miz Mozetta.

"You'll have a front-row seat," said Cap.

"But . . ." said Miz Mozetta.

"And you won't hurt yourself," Rudy said.

Miz Mozetta walked slowly back across the street.

"Night, all," she said to her friends, with a bit of a sniff. "My, I must be catchin' a cold."

She climbed up her steps and closed her door.

"Mm mm mm," said Mister Willie.

"Tsk tsk tsk," said Miz Lou Lillie.

Mister Brown just looked sad.

Up in her parlor, Miz Mozetta sighed. She turned on her scratchy old radio, sat by the window, and closed her eyes. The Fat Cat Band was playing and swaying, tooting and honking.

Before long, the music lifted her up and laid a road full of twinkling notes at her feet. Floating like a bubble, she followed them back to a summer night at the Blue Pearl Ballroom, long ago.

Everyone was doing the jitterbug, wild and free.

Miz Mozetta's feet itched to get out there and kick, kick, stomp, stomp, skiddle dee wee bop.

Bop, BOP! went a knock at the parlor door.

Poof! went the Blue Pearl Ballroom and everyone in it.

"Oh, horse sugar! Who can that be, spoiling my dream?" Miz Mozetta huffed.

She flung open her parlor door and in stepped Wildcat Willie. His hair was shiny and slick and blacker than black and smelled like shoe polish. "How do you do?" he said, swatting at a moth that flew out of his pocket.

Tap, tap. "Hullo hullo," said the lovely Lightnin' Lou Lillie. "Ow!" she said. "These shoes pinch!"

Rap, bap! It was Downtown Brown, in a cool-cat hat and dark glasses. He bowed to Miz Mozetta. "Wanna dance?"

Miz Mozetta's smile lit up the parlor. "Did somebody say dance?"

She turned up the radio, and faster than a rat can scat, up popped the Fat Cat Band, rooty toot toot and a re bop she bam.

Miz Mozetta leaped to the sound. Lightnin' Lou Lillie kicked off her slippers and stomped. Wildcat Willie whirled.

"Hey, cool!" Cap and Rudy stood in the doorway, snapping their fingers.

"Who invited you?" sniffed Lightnin' Lou.

"We heard the music," said Cap. "Is that you, Miz Lou Lillie?"

"Lightnin' Lou to you, bub," she said.

Cap and Rudy stared at their neighbors. "You all look different."

"You little ones scoot," said Downtown Brown. "Can't you see we're dancin' here?"

"But we want to learn that dance you're doing," said Rudy.

"Learn the jitterbug? Hmmph!" said Lightnin' Lou. "Can you do this?" She took a flying leap and—hoopla!—landed in Wildcat Willie's waiting arms.

"Uh . . ." said Rudy.

"Or this?" asked Downtown Brown. He spun himself so fast he disappeared.

"Wow," Cap said.

"Show us how, Miz Mozetta," begged Rudy. "Pretty please?"

Miz Mozetta thought it over. "Well . . ."

"They're too young," Wildcat Willie butted in.

"Too slow," frowned Downtown Brown.

"Hmmph!" said Lightnin' Lou, turning up her nose.

Cap and Rudy looked glum. "So long, then, Miz Mozetta," they said. The door slammed behind them.

Wildcat Willie turned the radio down and the band faded away. No one felt like whirling.

Or stomping. Or bebopping. Or anything.

"Something's missing," said Miz Lou Lillie.

"Oh, horse sugar!" said Miz Mozetta. "*Two* somethings are missing."

She dashed to the window. "Yoo-hoo, you two! Come back! Pretty please?"

"Do we get to jitterbug?" asked Cap and Rudy.

"Just like me," Miz Mozetta promised. "Turn up that radio, Wildcat!"

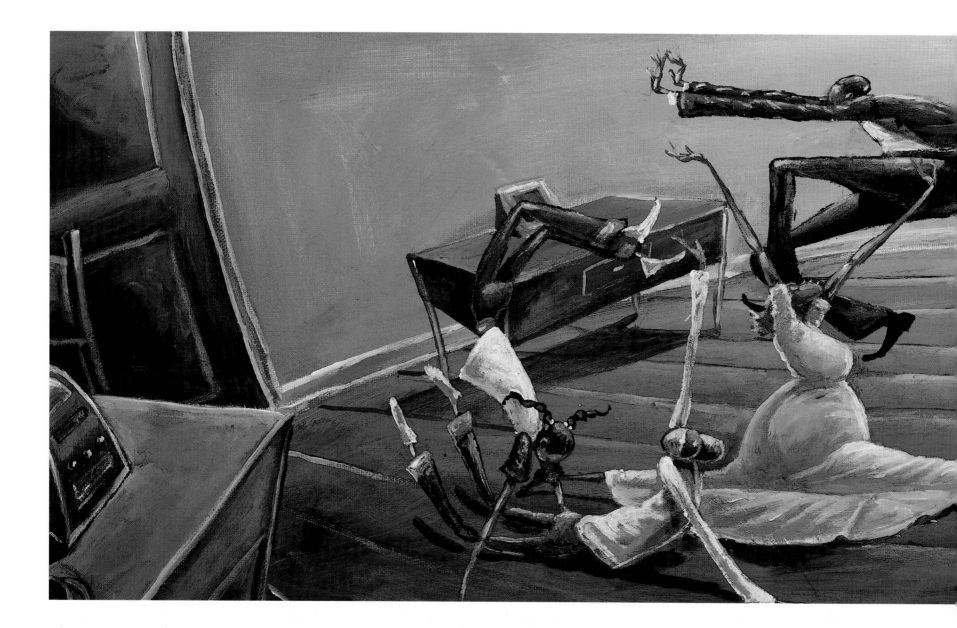

Wham! The Fat Cat Band came back, blasting. Miz Mozetta's parlor floor stretched out and back and away, shining like a new nickel.

"Look at that," Cap oohed.

The moon sent a stream of pearly blue light through the window.

"Man," Rudy aahed.

Miz Mozetta tapped out the beat. "Okay, young cats, let the beat hit your feet. Then close your eyes and just *swing* it. Hep, hep!"

Cap and Rudy closed their eyes.

"Hep, hep," everyone cried, and the parlor went jitterbug mad. Miz Mozetta was the maddest of all.

That night, her blue shoes were full of holes, but Miz Mozetta smiled as she set them under her bed.

"I believe I'll take a stroll uptown tomorrow," she told the moon with a yawn. "I need some new dancin' shoes."

Miz Mozetta snored all night, and dreamed . . . of red shoes. Her best color.